SLUMBER PARTY!

by Judith Caseley

Greenwillow Books, New York

Watercolor paints, colored pencils, and
a black pen were used for the full-color art.
The text type is Egyptian 505 Roman.

Library of Congress Cataloging-in-Publication Data
Caseley, Judith.
Slumber party! / Judith Caseley.
p.   cm.
Summary: Zoe's birthday party proves great fun
until bedtime, but Mama comes to the rescue and
the next day all agree it was the best sleepover ever.
ISBN 0-688-14015-7 (trade).
ISBN 0-688-14016-5 (lib. bdg.)
[1. Sleepovers—Fiction.   2. Birthdays—Fiction.]
I. Title.   PZ7.C2677Sl 1996   [E]—dc20
95-963   CIP   AC

To Jessica Swain, Sam, Melissa,
Jessica B., Samantha, Stephanie,
and especially Jenna!

Seven weeks before Zoe's birthday, Mama
said, "I've been thinking about your party."

"Can I have it at the circus?" Zoe asked.

"Too expensive," said Mama. "But how about an ice skating party?"

"No, thank you," Zoe said. "I don't want to fall down on my birthday."

"What about a ceramics party?"
asked her mother.
"I don't think so," Zoe told her.
"Sami had one, and so did Stephanie."

"An outdoors party?" said Mama.
"With a picnic and a birthday cake?"
"No, thanks," said Zoe. "The ants
and the bumblebees might ruin
my party."

"Bowling?" said Mama.
"Too noisy," Zoe told her.
"You can't hear them sing
'Happy Birthday to You.'"

"I give up," said Mama. Then her eyes lit up,
and she started to smile, and she said, "How
about a slumber party?"
Zoe's eyes lit up, and she started to smile,
and she said, "That's the one."

Zoe made four invitations. On each one she drew five girls in a bed and a cake with stars and hearts, and at the bottom she wrote, "Bring your own sleeping bag. RSVP."
And everybody said yes.

Melissa said she would bring a scary book
to read.
Stephanie said she was glad it wasn't another
ceramics party.
Jessica said she liked doughnuts for breakfast.
Sami said she had never been to a sleepover.

The day of the birthday party arrived.
Zoe wore her special party dress
that swirled when she twirled.

Mama and Papa took everyone down the street for pizza. After they ate, the waiters brought Zoe a chocolate cake with yellow roses on it, and everybody in the whole restaurant sang "Happy Birthday" to Zoe.

Then they all went next door to the drugstore, and each of the girls picked a nail polish for a manicure by Mama. Melissa and Stephanie chose Flaming Red, and Sami and Zoe liked Princess Pink, and Jessica said she couldn't wear nail polish to school, but she chose Outrageous Orange anyway.

When they got home, Mama put a basket of
rocks on the table, and the girls painted pictures
on them. Melissa made a cat, and Sami made
a monster, and Jessica made stripes, and
Stephanie made stars, and Zoe made a birthday
cake, but she could only fit four candles on it.

Melissa and Sami and Jessica and Stephanie
unpacked their suitcases and then crowded into
the bathroom with Zoe to brush their teeth.

They all unfolded their
sleeping bags and
laid them on the floor.
And that's when the
trouble began.
Melissa made a face,
and Stephanie covered
her eyes, and Jessica
said she wished it was
time for breakfast, and
Sami turned away.
Everybody wanted to
sleep next to Zoe.

"But I only have two sides," said Zoe.

By the time Sami started crying, Zoe had had an idea. If she slept on the couch, each of the others could have her head next to some part of Zoe's body.
So Melissa got Zoe's head, Jessica got her shoulders, Stephanie got her tummy, and Sami got her knees and toes. And everybody seemed happy, except maybe Sami, who was in the darkest part of the room and had nobody on the other side of her.

Mama stood over them and said, "Five sweet children," and Papa said, "Good night, birthday girl." They turned out all the lights except one, and they went into their bedroom and shut the door.

Melissa pulled a book out of her suitcase and
started to read. It was called <u>Very Scary Stories</u>,
and it was very very very scary.
Zoe heard little noises by her knees and toes.
It was Sami sobbing.
Then Jessica started to hiccup, and Melissa
stopped reading.
"Listen," Melissa whispered.

A low humming noise was
coming from the kitchen.
Melissa and Jessica and
Sami and Stephanie and
Zoe started screaming,
and they scrambled out
of their sleeping bags and
into Mama and Papa's room.
"What on earth is the matter?"
shouted Zoe's mother.
Everybody started speaking
at once, but mostly Zoe
heard the words, "I want
to go home."

So Zoe started crying the loudest of all.

Mama got out of bed and took them back to the
living room and said, "Into your sleeping bags."
Then she took the book of scary stories and put
it back in Melissa's suitcase and pulled a book
off the bookshelf and started to read.
The book was very funny, and one by one
the girls began to laugh, until they heard the
humming noise again, and Sami started gulping.
Mama said, "Girls, girls, girls. It's only the
refrigerator."

The five of them ran into the kitchen, and sure enough the refrigerator was humming.

Mama opened the refrigerator door and took out the milk and made hot chocolate for all of them.

Then they got back into bed, and only Jessica brushed her teeth, and Mama read the rest of the book to them.

The next day Zoe said she thought they fell asleep laughing.

And even though Mama forgot to give the girls manicures, and there were no doughnuts for breakfast, and Sami left her rabbit under the couch, everybody agreed that it was the best birthday party ever.

E
Cas

Caseley, Judith

Slumber party!

Bound to Stay Bound Books, Inc.